Yurek

LOOKING FOR LITTLE GREEN MEN

by Seth Jarvis

Illustrated by Nathan Y. Jarvis

Published by Capstone Press, Inc.

Distributed By

CP CHILDRENS PRESS®

CHICAGO

CIP

LIBRARY OF CONGRESS CATALOGING IN PUBLICATION DATA

Jarvis, Seth
Looking for little green men / by Seth Jarvis.
p. cm.-- (Star shows)
Summary: Discusses the requirements and likelihood of extraterrestrial life.

ISBN 1-56065-009-5

1. Life on other planets--Juvenile literature. [1. Life on other planets.] I.Title. II. Series.
QB54.J34 1989
574.999--dc20   **89-25148 CIP AC**

Designed by Nathan Y. Jarvis & Associates, Inc.

Capstone Press

Box 669, Mankato, MN, U.S.A. 56001

CONTENTS

SOMETHING TO THINK ABOUT

LOOK UP INTO a starry sky some evening. All around you are a zillion stars. Well, it *looks* like a zillion stars. Each star is a sun, not too different from ours. Some are bigger than our sun, some are smaller. Some are older than our sun, and some are younger. All are stars. Do any of them have planets going around them? Planets that are like Earth?

Pick a star and look at it. Could somebody be living on a planet circling that star? Could they be looking into *their* night sky, and see our sun as a tiny bright dot? Could someone out there be wondering if *we* exist? What about planets in our own solar system like Mars or Venus? Could "little green men" be looking up into their night sky at the Earth, and wondering if anyone lives on that pretty, little blue planet?

ARE WE ALONE?

Are we alone? That seems to be a simple question. Does it have a simple answer? That's what this book will explore. This book is about the search for **extraterrestrial** life. Extra-terrestrial means from beyond Earth. The possibility of extraterrestrial life isn't just something in stories or movies. Many scientists think life really could exist beyond our world.

Is there life beyond Earth?

Just for the fun of it, suppose you knew *for sure* that the answer is, "No. Earth is the only planet in the universe on which there is life."

The universe has something like a hundred billion galaxies in it. Each **galaxy** is made of anywhere from a few million to hundreds of billions of stars. What if you knew that out of all those trillions upon trillions of stars, *ours* is the only one with a planet around it that has life. The universe is filled with so many things. Yet somehow, life exists only here. Life is unique to our world.

What a strange thought! Think about this: The universe doesn't have only one galaxy. It has billions. It doesn't have only one star. It has trillions. The Earth isn't the only planet in the universe. It isn't even the only planet in the solar system. There are other planets with atmospheres, storms, and volcanoes.

What if in all the universe, life existed only on Earth? Why should that be? Does that make life very special, or was it just an accident?

If you knew for a fact that we were alone in the universe, you'd probably have a hard time sleeping at night.

Now, just for the fun of it, think about this. Suppose that you knew for sure that there are other intelligent forms of life beyond Earth.

All of a sudden you are faced with lots of important questions. How many other kinds of life? Where are they? What are they like? What kinds of science, art, and sports do they have? Can we talk to them? *Should* we talk to them?

If you knew for a fact that we were *not* alone in the universe, you'd probably have a hard time sleeping at night.

Either way, if you knew for sure the answer to the question, "Are we alone?" you'd have a lot to think about.

AN OLD QUESTION

People have wondered about life on other worlds for a long time. 2,000 years ago, a Roman poet named Lucretius wrote about it: "Nature is not unique to the visible world; we must have faith that in other regions of space there exist other earths, inhabited by other people and animals."

Around 1600 A.D. an Italian named Giordano Bruno wondered if life on other worlds was possible. He knew that our Earth went around the sun. Bruno thought other stars could also have planets going around them. He even said there could be life on those planets. The world wasn't ready to hear Giordano Bruno's ideas. He was burned at the stake because of his unpopular beliefs.

Then the telescope was invented. People began to look at the planet Mars. They saw that Mars has polar ice caps. These ice caps shrink and grow with the seasons, just like on Earth. People saw things on Mars that seemed to change over time. Could Mars be home to intelligent creatures? It seemed like a reasonable idea.

In 1820, a mathematician named Carl Gauss got an idea. He thought of a way to signal people who might live on Mars. He wanted to plant a giant area of land in a special pattern. The center of the pattern would be a huge triangle of light-colored wheat fields. On each side of the triangle he would plant squares of dark forests. The triangle and the squares around it would show an important mathematical idea. It is called the **Pythagorean Theorem**. Martians would look through their telescopes at Earth. They would see that people lived here who knew about mathematics.

In 1840, a man named Joseph von Littrow thought of another way to communicate with people on Mars. He wanted to dig a huge round trench in the Sahara Desert. This trench would be filled with millions of gallons of kerosene and set ablaze each night. (In 1840 people didn't worry about air pollution.) Martians would look at our planet. They would see a small bright circle of light. It would be a sign that people lived here.

In 1869, a man named Charles Cros thought of an easier (and cleaner) way to signal Martians. Cros wanted to place seven giant mirrors across Europe. They would form the pattern of the Big Dipper. The real Big Dipper can be seen from Mars. Martians would look through their telescopes. They would see a familiar pattern of twinkling lights on Earth. It would be a sign that people who knew about constellations lived here.

These were all attempts to contact extraterrestrials. They all used visible light. Near the start of the 20th century, a new form of "invisible" light was developed. It was called **radio**. Radio waves are like waves of light, but they have much less energy. Radio waves are "seen" with radio antennas connected to radio receivers.

In 1899, a scientist named Nikola Tesla tried to contact people in space. Tesla was a brilliant inventor. He was a pioneer in radio broadcasts. He sent a burst of radio waves into outer space. Then he listened to his receiver for a reply. He heard a strange whistling sound. He believed he had made contact with extraterrestrials! But it was only a type of radio noise called "whistlers." Whistlers are a natural radio signal made by ordinary flashes of lightning very far away.

A FORMULA FOR LIFE

Still the question remains. Are we alone? Can we know the answer?

We can make an educated guess. An astronomer named Frank Drake estimated the number of extraterrestrial neighbors we might have. First he thought of all the things that had to happen before we could look for extraterrestrials. Here's what he thought:

• Before you make contact with extraterrestrial life, you have to have the *science and technology* to explore space.

• Before you can use technology to explore space, you have to have *intelligence* to invent it.

• Before you can have intelligence, you have to have *life*.

• What do you need before life can exist? Life needs a planet. The planet can't be too cold or too hot. It can't be too big or too small. The planet should have some kind of air, but not too little or too much. It needs the right kinds of chemicals. It also needs lots of time for the chemicals to mix with each other. Life needs a planet that is **habitable.**

• Where do you find habitable planets? Around stars of course. But not all stars have planets. You need *stars with planets* circling around them.

Not just any star with planets will do, though. You need a certain kind of star. If the star is too big, it will only shine for a hundred million years or so. That's not long enough. Humans didn't appear until the Earth was about four and a half *billion* years old.

If the star is too small, the temperature won't be right to keep a planet just warm enough. The chances of having the right kind of planet orbit at just the right distance are very small.

Stars that are unstable won't work either. Life on a planet needs a steady amount of heat and light. Some stars pulse and are always changing the amount of energy they make. Unstable stars are not likely to have a planet with life around them.

A lot of stars circle around other stars. That's not very good for planets. A planet would always have to be the right distance from each star so that it stays at the right temperature. You need to look for stars that are by themselves.

• Finally, you've got to have *lots of stars*, all kinds of stars, together for a long time. Then they can make the chemicals that make planets and life possible.

All of these things are steps to making an intelligent form of life. We've been traveling backward though. We began with the last step (intelligent life) and ended at the first step (stars). Let's look at the steps again, only this time in their correct order. To have intelligent life begin in the universe, you must have:

1) Lots of stars together for a long time making the chemicals that make planets and life.

2) Stable stars that are medium-size and not too close to any other stars.

3) Planets around the star.

4) A habitable planet around the star.

5) The beginning of life on the habitable planet.

6) Non-intelligent life becoming intelligent life.

7) Intelligent life creating science and technology.

1.

2.

3.

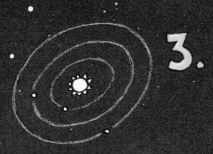

LIFE FORMS
WELCOME!

4.

5.

6.

MAKING YOUR OWN GUESS

Now you can estimate how likely it is that we have neighbors in space. How? Start at the top. Make an educated guess about how often each step takes place.

The first step says you need lots of stars together. No problem there. Our galaxy, the **Milky Way**, probably has around 400 billion stars. That's the number four with 11 zeros after it! The Milky Way is about 10 billion years old. That's plenty long enough for the right chemicals to be made.

The second step says you need stable, medium-size stars. They can't be in orbit around other stars. Astronomers think that maybe one star out of 10 fits that description.

The third step says the star has to have planets around it. Astronomers think that planets are fairly common around stars.

Astronomers think that as many as half the stars in the galaxy may have planets around them.

The fourth step says one of the planets has to be habitable. From here on, the estimates will be harder to make. How many habitable planets might be around a stable star? Let's look at our solar system as an example. Only one planet is habitable. Earth. Mars probably could have life on it, but we don't know. That means our star, the sun, has one or maybe two habitable planets. Let's say that every stable star has one or two habitable planets. That seems like a safe guess.

The fifth step says there must be life on the planet. Now the guesses are even harder to make. How can you estimate how often life occurs on habitable planets? Let's look at Earth. Life has been on Earth for most of our planet's history. Scientists have found that small, simple chemicals will join fairly easily with each other. They make larger, more complicated chemicals. These chemicals make life possible. It *seems* that life will begin almost as soon as it finds a healthy place to start.

This is just our Earth though. Will life

begin so quickly on other planets? The answer is probably yes, but let's play it safe. Let's say that life gets a start on only one out of every one hundred habitable planets. That means 99 out of a hundred planets are "duds."

The sixth step says non-intelligent life has to become intelligent. How likely is it that that will happen? Let's look at the Earth again. Life needs food, water, shelter, and warmth to stay alive. Smart animals can get these things better than dumb animals can. Smart animals will survive. Dumb animals will die. So animals will keep getting smarter and smarter.

Scientists study the remains of animals that died millions of years ago. These are called **fossils**. Scientists compare their brains to the sizes of their bodies. They have found that the sizes of animal brains kept getting bigger and bigger. That probably means life kept getting smarter and smarter.

It looks as if life just naturally gets smarter. But again, let's play it safe. Let's say that life on only one planet in a hundred becomes intelligent. The other 99 planets just have plants and animals that don't think.

The seventh and last step says intelligent

life must create science and technology. Without it, the intelligent life can't look for life beyond their world. It seems intelligence and technology go hand-in-hand. But then again, maybe they don't. What if the planet with intelligent life was completely covered with deep water? The intelligent life there might be like dolphins or whales. They could be very smart, but they wouldn't be able to build a rocket or a radio. Perhaps there are places where there are very smart people. But maybe they just don't have any interest in science and technology. How likely is this? Who knows? Let's play it safe again. Let's say that only one out of a hundred of the worlds with intelligent life explores space.

ADDING UP THE NUMBERS

Things get very interesting at this point. We have just made some guesses about how often things happen. Maybe somewhere all seven of those things have happened. That means there *should* be intelligent life there. There *should* be people who can explore space.

Now let's add our estimates together. We'll see what number we come up with.

First we said only one star in 10 was the right kind of star. There are 400 billion stars in the galaxy. That means there are 40 billion of the right kind of stars.

Next we said that about half of those stars might have planets. Half of 40 billion is 20 billion. Twenty billion stars with planets around them. A star with planets around it is a solar system. That would make about 20 *billion* solar systems in the galaxy!

Then we said that one or two planets in each solar system would be habitable. Let's say the number is only one, just to be safe. Twenty billion stars, each with one habitable planet, is 20 billion habitable planets. That's a lot!

Next we estimated that life happened on only one in a hundred of those habitable planets. One-hundredth of 20 billion is 200 million. Imagine, 200 million planets with life on them!

Now we have 200 million planets with life on them. We guessed that only one in a hundred would have intelligent life. One-hundredth of 200 million is 2 million. Two million worlds with intelligent life! Amazing!

Finally, we estimated that only one in a hundred of those worlds would have intelligent people who could create science and technology. Only one in a hundred might make contact with us. One-hundredth of 2 million is 20,000. Twenty thousand extraterrestrial civilizations that could make contact with us! It boggles the mind!

So why hasn't someone contacted us by now?

Because there is a catch. (Wouldn't you know it?) *When* are those 20,000 extraterrestrial civilizations in our galaxy? What if they all died a million years ago and we are the only ones left? What if we are the first of the 20,000 and the rest won't show up for a million years?

NOT ENOUGH TIME?

Time becomes the real problem. What if there *are* intelligent forms of life on other planets? How can we know how long they are around? More important, how can we know how long they would be able to contact us? We have a name for the length of time extra-terrestrials can contact other life. It's called their Space Age.

How long can anyone's Space Age last? One hundred years? A thousand years? A million years? Let's say an average Space Age lasts a million years. That would mean we might have dozens of neighbors in space.

Dozens of neighbors. Is that an accurate count? Probably not. We might have made some mistakes in our estimates. Maybe life starts on 99 out of a hundred habitable planets, not just one. Or maybe it happens on only one in a million.

Our guess could be a lot bigger. It could be a lot smaller. We do know there's at least one: us. The number could just as easily be a thousand.

TOO FAR AWAY?

For fun, let's say that there *are* a thousand different forms of extraterrestrial intelligence in our galaxy with us right now.

Wow! A thousand! They should be all over the galaxy!

Not necessarily. Our galaxy has 400 billion stars. For every star that has life on one of its planets, there are 400 million stars that don't. That's only one "hit" for every 400 million "misses." The distance between those stars could be hundreds of light-years. A **light-year** is the distance light travels in a year. That means that it could take hundreds of years for light to travel from one solar system to another. And our rockets can't go as fast as the **speed of light**. In a rocket, such a trip would take millions of years.

But suppose that extraterrestrials could travel faster than we can. Would they come here? If they were a few hundred light-years away, they wouldn't see anything very interesting about our sun. It's just an ordinary star.

But if they were a little closer, say 50 light-years away, they might notice something odd about our sun. They would pick up radio signals from one of its planets. These radio signals would not be like any of the ones that happen naturally in space. They would say strange things like, "TWA flight 552, you are cleared to land runway seven." The extraterrestrials would be hearing radio broadcasts from Earth. *That* would make our solar system worth investigating!

RADIO MESSAGES

It turns out that Nikola Tesla was on the right track. Radio broadcasts from Earth are probably the best way of contacting extraterrestrials. Quite by accident, we've been announcing our existence into space since the early 1900's. Our radio broadcasts spill out into space all the time. They spread out in all directions at the speed of light.

Suppose some extraterrestrials heard radio messages from Earth. What would they do?

It is very hard to guess. Sending a space ship to visit us would be the *most* difficult thing to do. Why? The distance would be so great. Even traveling at the speed of light (which is probably impossible), it would take them many years to make the trip.

And what if they did come in a space

ship? Would they be able to shake hands with us? That is very unlikely. Chances are they wouldn't be able to breathe our air. Also, we might catch some strange disease from them. Or they might catch one from us. Direct contact might be too risky. It might be just too much trouble to make the trip.

There's a better way, though. Radio broadcasts. Radio waves travel at the speed of light. They can travel just about anywhere in space. They are also cheap. A dollar's worth of electricity can send a 60-word telegraph message across the galaxy at the speed of light. A whole encyclopedia could easily be radioed to extraterrestrials who were 50 light-years away.

Now we come to a difficult question. Is anyone out there trying to make radio contact with us? Let's say there are a few hundred kinds of intelligent extraterrestrial life in our galaxy. Could we "hear" their radio signals?

MANY OBSTACLES

Even if we *knew* that someone was out there trying to send us a radio message, we are faced with several big problems.

Let's say you've got a powerful radio receiver. You want to use it to find extraterrestrial radio messages being sent to Earth. A regular antenna like on a car radio or a walkie-talkie won't work. It isn't powerful enough to pick up a very faint radio message. Your radio must have a powerful and sensitive receiver. It needs a dish-antenna, like the ones used to receive satellite TV signals.

You need a **radio telescope**. An ordinary telescope helps you see things far away. It collects and focuses light into an eyepiece. A radio telescope collects and focuses radio waves from a dish-antenna into a receiver. Radio telescopes can work both at night and during the day. They can even work when there are clouds overhead. That's because radio waves can pass through clouds.

Radio telescopes can pick up extremely faint radio signals. However, they must be pointed directly at the source of the signal. Otherwise they won't hear it.

Here's the first problem. Where do you aim your radio telescope? There are around a thousand stars that might be home to life. You can't aim your antenna at a thousand stars at the same time. You'll have to look at them one by one.

Now you have another problem. What radio "station" do you listen to? Look at the dial of a regular radio. There are dozens of radio stations on the dial. Radio messages from outer space could be broadcast on any one of a hundred *million* different channels.

Even if you have your antenna pointed at the right place, you might not be tuned to the right channel.

And there's another problem. Suppose you have your antenna pointed in the right direction. It's tuned to the right channel. But while you are listening, the extraterrestrials aren't sending a signal! *When* you listen is important, too.

Let's say you are a scientist. You are looking for signs of extraterrestrial life. You have carefully picked out a thousand stars you want to look at. You have only a year to look. You would have to look at two or three stars each day of the year. No weekends off, no holidays, no vacations. You'd only have eight or 12 hours to look at each star. That's not very long. During those hours, you'd have to tune your radio to millions of different channels. You'd have to hope that you'd hit the right channel at the right moment.

What if a message from extraterrestrials arrived the day before you pointed your radio telescope in their direction? Or the day after? Then you would never know they were there.

Fortunately, scientists are figuring out better ways to listen to the stars for radio messages. New computers can listen to millions of radio channels at the same time. Computers can also move the radio telescope's antenna from one star to another. The astronomers don't even have to be there.

Now suppose you've searched for a long time. One day a radio telescope finds a signal from a race of extraterrestrials. Wow! Even before we tried to understand the message, we have learned something very important. We are not alone.

UNDERSTANDING MESSAGES FROM SPACE

What of the message itself? Would it be hard to figure out? Scientists don't think so. They think the message will probably be easy to understand.

An alien message might be like this:

"Beep, (pause), Beep, Beep, (pause), Beep, (pause), (pause), Beep, and so on. The message would be a series of beeps and pauses. This is called a **binary message.** Binary is a type of counting. There are only two numbers, zero and one (or beep and pause). It's the simplest form of counting possible. Each 1 and 0, or beep and pause, of a binary number is called a "bit." If you want to send a message that just about anyone can understand, you send it in binary code. The binary message you heard with your radio telescope would look like this:

1,0,1,1,0,1,0,0,1, and so on.

Let's say a message we received on Earth from extraterrestrials looked like this:

01001010010010010000100100101001001011101001001001010010010010101000001001010010

This message is made of 77 ones and zeros. The message is 77 "bits" long. What do they mean? Think about what you know about the message. Right now all you know for sure is that it contains 77 bits of binary code. Seventy-seven is an interesting number though. Here's why.

Seventy-seven is a number that you get when you multiply two prime numbers together. A prime number is a number that can be evenly divided only by itself and one. The number 16 is *not* a prime number. You can evenly divide 16 by one, two and four.

16÷1=16

16÷2=8

16÷4=4

The number 17 *is* a prime number. You can only divide it evenly by itself and one.

17÷1=17

You get 77 by multiplying two prime numbers together: 7 and 11.

7 x 11=77

Why is this important? It's important because the 7 and 11 give you new ways to arrange the message. One way is a grid with seven rows and eleven columns. The other way is a grid of eleven rows and seven columns.

Now let's lay out these grids. We'll fill up each grid with the 1s and 0s of the message. Put the first number of the message in the upper left of the grid. Then keep filling in the squares, left-to-right, top-to-bottom. One way, with eleven rows down and seven columns across looks like this:

0	1	0	0	1	0	1
0	0	1	0	0	1	0
0	1	0	0	0	0	1
0	0	1	0	0	1	0
1	0	0	1	0	0	1
1	1	1	0	1	0	0
1	0	0	1	0	0	1
0	1	0	0	1	0	0
1	0	0	1	0	1	0
0	0	0	0	1	0	0
1	0	1	0	0	1	0

11

7

Now let's try another idea. Make every square of the grid with a 1 on it a black square. Leave the squares with 0s blank. You get a pattern like this:

That doesn't look very interesting. Let's try arranging the grid the other way, seven rows down and eleven columns across. Fill in the numbers of the message and you'll get this:

0	1	0	0	1	0	1	0	0	1	0
0	1	0	0	1	0	0	0	0	1	0
0	1	0	0	1	0	1	0	0	1	0
0	1	1	1	1	0	1	0	0	1	0
0	1	0	0	1	0	1	0	0	0	0
0	1	0	0	1	0	1	0	0	1	0
0	1	0	0	1	0	1	0	0	1	0

7

← 11 →

Now make the 1s black and leave the 0s blank. What do you see? The message! The extraterrestrials are saying, "Hi!" OK, so it wasn't much of a message. But now you understand the idea.

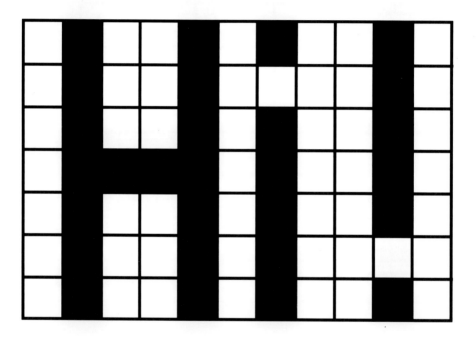

Most of the radio waves leaving Earth are from radio, TV, and radar transmitters that spill into outer space. They're not sent into space on purpose. Once, on November 16, 1974, Earth sent a message of greetings into outer space on purpose. It came from a giant radio telescope in Puerto Rico called the Arecibo Radio/Radar Observatory. It sent a string of 1,679 bits toward a large group of stars called M13. The stars in M13 are about 25,000 light-years away.

The number 1,679 can be made by multiplying two prime numbers together, 73 and 23.

73 x 23 = 1,679

Just like our 77-bit message, the bits of this message can be arranged into a grid. Instead of a word though, this message creates a simple picture.

This one picture contains a lot of information about us. It shows that life on Earth is made of hydrogen, oxygen, nitrogen, and phosphorous. It shows how the chemicals are arranged together. It shows a rough picture of what a human looks like. It describes how tall a human is. The picture shows that Earth is the third of nine planets around our sun. It shows how many people live on that planet. The picture even has a rough drawing of the radio telescope that sent the message.

That's a lot of information for only 1,679 bits! A picture really *is* worth a thousand words.

Will anyone receive this message? It's hard to say. We do know that it will take about 25,000 years to get where it's going. Perhaps someone out there *will* receive it and send back a reply. It will take another 25,000 years to get back here. In other words, we shouldn't expect a reply for about 50,000 years.

If we do someday discover that we have "neighbors" in space, we will learn things we cannot even imagine today. But what if we don't make contact? The search itself will have told us a lot.

We will have learned a lot about the stars around us. We will also have learned how rare life is. That alone is worth knowing.

A wonderful thing happens when you try to answer the question, "Am I alone?" You begin to answer another question, "Who am I?"

GLOSSARY

Binary message: A message made from only two signals, such as a beep and a pause.

Extraterrestrial: Something that comes from a place other than Earth.

Fossil: The remains of animals and plants that died millions of years ago.

Galaxy: A large group of stars held together by gravity.

Habitable: Having the right combination of atmosphere, warmth, light, and chemicals to make life possible.

Light-year: The distance that a beam of light can travel in a year. A light year is equal to about six trillion miles, or nine and a half trillion kilometers.

Milky Way: Giant spiral-shaped galaxy of about 400,000,000,000 (400 billion) stars. Galaxies come in a wide variety of shapes and sizes.

Pythagorean theorem: A mathematical formula about the relationship of the size of the squares that can be placed on the three sides of a right triangle.

Radio: A form of electromagnetic energy that has far less energy than visible light. Radio waves are easy to make, easy to receive, and travel at the speed of light.

Radio telescope: A piece of equipment that collects and focuses radio waves into a very sensitive receiver. Most radio telescopes use a dish antenna to focus radio waves.

Speed of light: The fastest that the laws of nature allow anything to travel through the universe. The speed of light is 186,300 miles (300,000 kilometers) per second.